GIRLS SURVIVE

Girls Survive is published by Stone Arch Books
A Capstone Imprint
1710 Roe Crest Drive
North Mankato, Minnesota 56003
www.mycapstone.com

Cataloging-in-Publication Data is available on the Library of Congress website.
ISBN: 978-1-4965-7852-5 (library binding)
ISBN: 978-1-4965-8012-2 (paperback)
ISBN: 978-1-4965-7857-0 (eBook PDF)

Summary:
In 1941, Alice's days are filled with swimming in the Hawaiian sea, going to school, and helping watch her younger siblings. But on December 7, everything changes when Japan bombs Pearl Harbor and brings the United States into World War II. Within hours Alice's father, a Japanese immigrant, is collected by authorities and sent to an internment camp. Meanwhile, Alice is left behind to face discrimination from former friends.

Designers:
Heidi Thompson and Charmaine Whitman

Cover art:
Alessia Trunfio

Image credits:
Shutterstock: Curly Pat, Design Element, kaokiemonkey, Design Element, Max Lashcheuski, Design Element; XNR Productions, 109

Author's Dedication:
For my mother and my grandparents.
Okage sama de: I am what I am because of you.

Printed and bound in the United States of America.
PA62

ALICE ON THE ISLAND

A Pearl Harbor Survival Story

by Mayumi Shimose Poe

illustrated by Matt Forsyth

STONE ARCH BOOKS
a capstone imprint

CHAPTER ONE

Pālolo, Hawai'i
November 8, 1941
Saturday morning, 8 a.m.

I became aware of the time and day slowly. Our house was old. It had a tin roof, so when it rained, you would hear every little sound. *Pon. Pon. Pon. Pono-pono-pono. Pon. Pon. Pon. Pon.* Opening my eyes, I listened to the noises.

But it wasn't the rain that woke me that day. It was the silence. I was used to the commotion of my younger siblings, five-year-old Momo and two-year-old Ken. They were always running around and making noise. But today it was quiet. Where were they, and what were they up to?

I quickly went from peacefully resting on my futon to wrestling the mattress back into its folded position. I couldn't help but wonder what kind of trouble Momo and Ken were getting into.

The rain went from drips to a downpour—or at least that's what I thought at first. But through the open window, I saw a flock of birds rush by. It wasn't the rain I'd heard, but the beating of wings. The Midoris, the couple who lived at the end of the block, kept homing pigeons. It was always a thrill to watch the birds burst and swoop, free in the sky.

Someone in the kitchen had turned on the radio, and the soft finger picking of a ukulele blended with the sounds of rain. The musician began to play a tender song.

I could now hear other sounds too. There, faintly, was Mama's voice, followed by the louder, clashing sounds of Momo. Then Mama again, gently shushing her.

I heard someone walking in the yard outside our room, then the snips of cutters. Papa was outside tending his bonsai plants like he did every Saturday. He watered them regularly. But he could only fuss over them on the weekends when he wasn't working at *Nippu Jiji*, the Japanese-language newspaper.

Today wasn't just *any* Saturday. Today, November 8, 1941, was my thirteenth birthday. I pulled on an old, favorite dress—black with tiny pink roses and heart-shaped buttons. Turning to the mirror, I wondered, *What does thirteen look like?*

On the one hand, I knew I couldn't have completely changed overnight. On the other hand, I believed the world was filled with possibilities.

But there I was, with the same chin-length brown hair, same dark eyes, same bushy caterpillar brows. My adult-sized teeth still looked too large for my mouth. I was still as thin as a bamboo shoot, with awkward, long legs and neck.

Heading for the doorway, I did my best movie star look—chin low, smile shy, but eyes bright and wide—and gazed into the mirror. Almost instantly I rolled my eyes, having seen the goofy result.

We can't all be Pearly, I told myself. I was thinking of my glamorous older sister with her glossy black hair and ruby-red lips.

Following the sounds of Mama's voice, I found her, Momo, and Ken on the porch by the front yard. They were reading from a stack of picture books, which explained the quiet. The screen banged closed, announcing me, and Ken-chan sang out, "Happy Birthday!" as if he'd been holding it in for hours. Maybe he had been.

Papa came around the corner from the side yard. He held his cutters in one hand.

"Sun's been up awhile and finally you too?" he said. I couldn't see his face under the wide brim of his straw hat. But I could hear his smile.

"Well, you turned off my double alarm clock," I said, referring to my younger siblings.

"They decided to go off in our room instead," Papa said. "That was a present for you, Alice. Happy birthday."

Mama clucked her disapproval and moved the kids off her lap. "A birthday *treat*, anyway. There'll be others."

Bang went the screen again. Then just as soon—our house was not that big—Mama was back with a beautiful strand of *puakenikeni* flowers in her hands to drape around my neck.

"Happy birthday, Alice," she said.

The blossoms were the softest, creamiest white you could imagine, and the smell was like ripe cantaloupe and honey.

"*Arigatogozaimasu*, Mama," I said, giving her my thanks in Japanese. I ducked my head, which dipped me further into the sweet scent.

"Well," Papa murmured. "I guess I'd better finish." He thumbed his finger in the direction of the side yard. "Then I can get cleaned up so I can be seen in public with my pretty gals."

I walked with Papa back toward the side yard. "What are you working on today?" I asked. I was always curious about Papa's green thumb.

"Ah, today it is something very special," Papa said with a gentle smile.

Among Papa's collection, a new plant stood out. My eyes settled on a small azalea tree in full bloom. It was a perfect example of all Papa had learned about the art of bonsai. Its slender, curving trunk opened like a pink parasol over a small wood carving of a girl in a blue dress.

"I call it Alice," he said.

"Oh, Papa," I said, throwing myself at him.

"Honey, I'm all dirty," he protested, but he still hugged me anyway. "Anyway, happy birthday."

"Yes, happy thirteenth, Ali-chan!" a voice called over the sound of feet crunching up our gravel drive.

I couldn't believe it. Even Pearly and my older brother, Yosh, were home today. Soon my big sister was hugging me.

"What are you guys doing here?" I asked. Pearly and Yosh lived in an apartment in Mōʻiliʻili, a short drive away from our home. It was near Pearly's job as a nurse at Queen's Hospital and Yosh's classes at the university and his ROTC duties.

"Oh, we were just . . . in the neighborhood," Yosh said as he slowly moved closer to Pearly and me. "Just dropping by." He stalked closer. I giggled in anticipation. "Just thinking about . . . a *puppy pile*!"

I shrieked as Yosh crushed Pearly and me. Recognizing the game, Momo and Ken squealed and pushed their way into the middle of the huddle. And despite the dirt on him, Papa grasped each of Mama's hands, tightly encircling us all.

Mama shook her head, but a small smile played around her mouth. She let Papa hold her hands for a moment before she pulled herself free.

"Enough already, Yosh, you're messing up my hair," scolded Pearly. Yosh squeezed us so hard we groaned, and then he released us. "Anyway, Ali," Pearly added, "we wouldn't miss your thirteenth for the world."

She tucked a loose curl behind her ear, along with a blossom that had fallen to the grass from a nearby flowering tree. She leaned like a movie star against the strong trunk of the tree, and I wanted nothing more than to know how to lean against a tree like that.

"I know I seem old to you"—everyone laughed—"but I still remember turning thirteen. It's really special, Ali. You're right on the brink," Pearly said.

CHAPTER TWO

Pālolo, Hawai'i
December 7, 1941
Sunday morning, 8:30 a.m.

"Alice." The word came to me as if through a fog. "Alice. Alice."

"Yes, Ken-chan?" I whispered to my little brother, not looking up from my book.

It was early still. I had been lying on my futon in the dark, not wanting to turn on a light or even get up to use the bathroom because the floorboards creaked. Momo was still asleep, and I was hoping that Ken might go back to bed so I could keep reading.

"Plane!" he cried.

"Oh, you saw a plane?" I asked.

Ken was kneeling on the futon he shared with Momo, his blanket tangled at the foot of the bed. He nodded excitedly. My brother loved planes . . . and trucks, trains, cars, and boats.

"What did it look like?" I asked, placing my open book facedown on my mattress to hold my page. Ken took this as an invitation and came over to sit on my lap. "Green plane. Red dot." He jabbed a plump finger toward the window.

I couldn't see a thing. The clouds over the mountains were a heavy knit of gray.

"More?" Ken asked hopefully.

"Must be the Navy doing drills. Should we go outside and see what we can see?" I asked.

When he nodded, I set him on my hip and tiptoed from the room. I left the bedroom door open so that when Momo woke, she wouldn't have to wrestle with the doorknob.

In the hall outside our room, I opened the screen door to the side yard. I could hear the radio softly playing Hawaiian music in the kitchen and Mama humming along.

Ken-chan and I walked past the shaded rows of Papa's bonsai to the backyard, where a ladder leaned up against the house. I had climbed it often, to scoop mango leaves from the rain gutters or to take in displays of fireworks during the Lunar New Year. Momo and Ken weren't allowed on the roof, but on a few, rare occasions I had taken them up.

Today I had Ken-chan go first, and I followed a couple rungs behind. Our eyes were already turned skyward, so when the plane came through the clouds, we saw it right away. We stopped where we were, almost at the top of the ladder.

This plane was white, but it still had the red dot my brother had described. It was more of a circle than a dot.

It was the red sun on the white flag of Japan, Mama's homeland.

"Plane." Ken nodded, satisfied.

The plane swooped for a moment, its nose pointed toward Honolulu. Then, still covered in morning fog, it was gone again. A ghostship plane.

I blinked hard in the strange light. I recognized the red sun symbol, but I didn't understand what a Japanese plane would be doing in the skies above O'ahu. I felt a sudden uneasiness.

Ken-chan had started climbing the last few rungs, eager to climb onto the roof and look for more planes. I stopped him with a hand on his lower back. "Let's go find Mama and get you some snackies!" I said. An offer of snacks always worked.

As we climbed down, I took a longer look at the sky and realized that what I had thought was fog was, in fact, smoke. Big, dark clouds loomed to the west, over the base at Pearl Harbor, lit by rapid white bursts.

As Ken-chan and I walked past the bonsai again, I realized the music I'd heard earlier had stopped. Instead, I heard the high, thin buzzing of the planes approaching the base, followed by low booms. I scooped Ken-chan back up and hurried around to the front of the house, entering the kitchen. Mama stood with her back to us.

"Mama?" I called. She turned and took us both in her arms.

Instead of music, the DJ Webley Edwards was on the air, a strange tone to his voice. Normally he spoke with a smooth, soothing tone, introducing live music about hula dancers and flowers. Today he didn't sound like himself at all.

"All right now, listen carefully," the DJ said. "The island of O'ahu is being attacked by enemy planes. The center of this attack is Pearl Harbor, but planes are attacking airfields as well. This is not a drill. All military and police personnel, report for duty."

Mama held Ken-chan and me tightly, and Webley's words kept coming too quickly. "Keep off the streets unless you have a duty to perform. Keep under cover and keep calm. Keep your radio on, but don't use your phone unless absolutely necessary, as they are needed for emergency calls."

The voice on the radio became lower and graver as he added, "The mark of Japan has been seen on these planes. Many of you have been asking if this is a maneuver. This is not a maneuver. This is the real McCoy."

The words were in English, but I couldn't make sense of them. *What was a McCoy, and what was the difference between a real and fake one? Why was Japan bombing my home?* I felt confused and afraid.

"Papa?" Mama called from the kitchen, hurrying to my father's closed office door. I followed, Ken still in my arms.

Mama called out again, this time saying "Shiroku," Papa's first name. Her formality took my breath away. In our family, Papa was almost always *Papa* and Mama was *Mama*. The use of his actual name showed me how upset she was.

Mama knocked hard and reached for the knob, but the door opened on its own. There Papa stood, fully dressed, down to his shoes. This was unheard of in our house, where shoes were always traded at the door for indoor-only slippers.

"*Gomenasai*, Mama," he said, meaning *I'm sorry*. His own radio was playing in the background. "I heard you the first time, but I was getting ready."

Getting ready for what? I worried.

Mama gaped at his clothes. "What's the meaning here?" she demanded.

"Chieko-san . . . ," Papa started to say. I noticed he'd used her first name too, but just then Momo threw open our bedroom door and interrupted him.

"Mama!" Momo cried out, rubbing her eyes angrily. She wasn't the baby of the family, but she sure seemed like it in the mornings.

She sat down hard on her butt, insisting, "MAMA!" But Mama just stared at Papa.

Ken-chan's eyes darted from Mama to Momo to Papa and around again, then held mine. He asked, "Momo mad? Momo sad?" His eyes were wet.

"Mamamamamamamamama!" Momo's voice was impossible to ignore. She began running toward us, her favorite doll in her arms.

"SHUSH UP!" Mama yelled.

Momo came to a full halt in shock, her little cheeks reddening. Ken's arms tightened around my neck.

Papa knelt down for Momo just as she started an enraged wail.

"MAMAAAAA!" Momo screamed but wrapped her chubby arms around Papa's neck.

“There, there, little peach. Little dumpling. Little one,” Papa crooned. He bounce-swayed Momo like he had when she was a baby, despite the sweat gathering at his brow. “Small bird. Ladybug. Kitten-mouse. Cherry pie. My whipped cream on top.”

Still swaying, Papa said, “Mama, I must go. I haven’t been able to reach Pearly or Yosh by telephone. I’m going to drive over to their apartment. And they’re going to need me at the office. There will be so many stories to report. I’m taking Alice with me. She can gather emergency supplies, and then either Pearly or I will drive her home. Ali, please go get dressed. Hurry now.”

CHAPTER THREE

Pālolo, Hawai'i
December 7, 1941
Sunday morning, 9:45 a.m.

Papa held my hand as we drove down Pālolo's main street, Wai'alae Avenue. He stayed five miles under the speed limit and obeyed every stop sign and red light. The streets were nearly empty of cars, except for parked ones.

Papa was smartest person I knew. Sitting alone with him, my questions spilled out. "Why is Japan attacking us? What's going to happen now?" I demanded.

I had felt so scared after Webley's grim broadcast and Mama and Papa's serious exchange.

But on the street, people walked dogs, headed into church, talked with their neighbors across fences. It seemed like a regular Sunday. I didn't know what to believe or feel. "Is it safe to be out here right now?" I asked.

Papa squeezed my hand. "I hate to say it, but it looks like America's being drawn into the war. The Japanese are attacking Pearl Harbor and the airfields so that America won't have a military stronghold in the Pacific. But there's nothing worth attacking on this side of the island." Papa nodded to himself, like he was convincing us both.

He continued, "We'll find Pearly and Yosh. You'll stay with them while I check in at the newspaper. Better prepare in case there's shortages of food or supplies. So, while you're waiting, please go to the store for Mama. If I can get away, I'll bring you home. Otherwise, your sister can."

Papa's matter-of-fact calmness helped me focus.

Once we reached Waiola Street and parked outside Pearly and Yosh's apartment, Papa let go of my hand. He fished his wallet out of his back pocket and rifled through it.

"Here," he said and handed me five crisp singles. "Try to pick up some canned goods, bottled water, batteries, propane for the camp stove. Some candles and a box of matches. Toilet paper. Like when it's hurricane season."

I had never held so much money before, and I felt very grown up to be trusted with it. It felt like a special moment that I wanted to sit in longer with Papa, but he was already out of the car, slamming his door.

"Hurry, Ali," he urged.

Pearly flung open the door before we reached it. Her face was bare, and her hair was pulled into a simple half-ponytail. I could feel Papa's relief as he pulled my sister into his arms.

"We couldn't get though on the phone. We were worried!" Papa cried. "Where's Yosh?"

"He's fine, Pa," Pearly replied. "His ROTC unit got called up for duty right after the attack began. Some of his buddies picked him up not too long ago. He said to tell Ma not to worry, but it might be a while before he can be in contact again."

"As if Mama won't worry." Papa shook his head.

"What do you make of all this, Papa?" Pearly asked. She seemed as young as me, asking Papa to help her understand what was happening. "They're saying the fleet at Pearl Harbor's been totaled and the bases at Wheeler, Hickam, and Kāneʻohe have been hit hard. That Japanese pilots and spies have been seen in the hills."

"I don't know much yet, Pearly. I need to check in at *Nippu Jiji*. After I go to the office, maybe I'll know more. Maybe not." Papa shrugged, seeming weary.

"I must go now," he added. "Alice is going to fetch emergency supplies. Maybe you should get some for you and Yosh too. I'll call or return as soon as I can." He hugged us each and headed back to the door. "It'll come out right in the end, you'll see. And if it doesn't, wait a little longer. Eventually it will."

Pearly nodded, but her brow did not relax. I was also unconvinced.

Not long after Papa left, Pearly's phone rang in the kitchen and she rose to answer it. After a beat, she turned to me and said, "Ali, it's work. I have to take this."

I tried to be patient, but I was sitting on the edge of my seat. My legs shook with nervousness, and my heart fluttered.

What does this attack mean? My mind raced with questions. *So Japan is wrecking our ships and planes, but when they are done, will they go away? Or will they stay? Will the islands become a territory of Japan instead of America?*

I couldn't just sit still in my sister's familiar living room while the world changed around me. I stuck my head into the kitchen and called out, "Pearly, I'm going to the store. I'll be right back."

Pearly placed her hand over the receiver and said, "I'll go with you. Just give me a few minutes."

"Pearly, it's right down the street. I'm not going to get lost. I'll be back real quick, I promise."

Her brow knitted with disapproval, my sister finally nodded.

It felt good to move. I knew this neighborhood well. I knew which streets would take me to the *hongwanji*, where we took Japanese language lessons, or to the Shinto shrine, where in summer we attended the *Obon* dance. I knew the way to the local noodle shop, the drugstore, and of course Koide Store.

As I walked down Waiola Street, my eyes saw the familiar, but what my ears heard was strange: distant booming, the *tikka-tikka-tikka* of gunfire, and what felt like dozens of sirens.

The Koides had opened the corner store the year before. It had quickly became Pearly and Yosh's go-to grocery stop. Today the tiny store was full of people. Everyone was rushing, muttering, grabbing, grumbling, muscling heavy baskets.

Soon I was behaving like everyone else, snatching cans of SPAM and green beans before the person behind me could. I was reaching for the last few packages of toilet paper when I heard a faint sound.

A whining, whirring noise grew closer and closer, to the point that it was uncomfortably loud. Before I could cover my ears, the sound exploded in a boom that sent the ground beneath my feet shuddering violently.

I staggered to keep my balance, knocking into Papa Koide. He automatically bowed and said, "Pardon me." Someone screamed, and grown-ups were crying.

My feet felt like they were stuck in cement. But inside, I felt panic rising. It felt like a nest of hornets swarming around right after a baseball bat has knocked down a hive.

My mind raced. *Papa said there was nothing worth attacking here. I thought I was safe. Now danger has found me, and I am alone.*

I wanted so badly to be with someone who loved me and could make things feel OK, even if they weren't. *Had Papa made it to the office? Was Yosh safe? Was our quiet little Pālolo block still safe for Mama and the kids, or were the planes now attacking everywhere? Where* was *Pearly?* As frightened as I was to move, I knew I had to find my sister. I dropped my basket and stood up.

Someone hissed at me, "Girl, stay *down*." But I hurried from the store. The hiss turned to a yell, "Eh, girl! Don't go! Somebody, don't let her go. We should all just stay *down*. Not safe."

Sirens were closing in. I hurried back down Waiola Street—toward Pearly's but also toward the sirens. A telephone pole had splintered and fallen, like a giant set of chopsticks, split wrong. Glass glinted on the sidewalk from a broken window. An older woman hunched over on the curb, a towel wrapped tightly to her arm. She was shivering, surrounded by red brown puddles of her own blood. My stomach lurched at the sight of the blood.

I asked, "You OK, auntie?"

She looked up, and I saw more blood along her forehead. "The window exploded," she said. "I was standing there, and it just . . . went explode."

"Someone with you? I can get my sister, she's a nurse," I said.

"No, no . . . my son went inside the house for get bandages. I was going too, but I got dizzy. He'll be back," the woman answered, taking my hand in hers. "But go to your sister. Not safe to be walking around alone right now."

I nodded and continued on my way. I was running now, so I felt the heat of the blaze before I saw it. Flames had engulfed several buildings at the intersection of McCully and King, catching on to the next structure and the next. I froze, uncertain of what to do. The heat was intense.

These familiar streets had been transformed into an obstacle course. The way back to Pearly was just a couple blocks before me, but I couldn't continue forward. The flames were still spreading, and my way was blocked by emergency vehicles. I could see another blaze across McCully Street. People were running toward the fire engines, yelling for firefighters.

An ambulance was parked partially on the sidewalk before me. Its driver rounded McCully, covered in grime. His arms were full of a bundle. When he laid it down on a stretcher, I saw it was a small girl. As small as Ken. She wasn't moving.

Then Pearly found me, coming from the direction of Koide Store. "*Alice Fujii*! What the heck is the matter with you? I've been looking absolutely everywhere!" My usually elegant older sister was breathing heavily and still wearing her tattered housedress. I threw myself at her, finally able to cry.

"There was an explosion," I sobbed. "I was in the store, and I almost fell over. And there's, like, three different fires. And a lady's window exploded, and she was bloody. And over there's a baby that . . ."

Tears stung my eyes, and I paused, trying not to let emotion cloud my voice. "I don't think she's OK, Pearly. Can you check? She's just a baby! Little, like Ken-chan. Where are her parents? The man took her in the ambulance, but they're not even driving!"

Pearly looked doubtfully over at the ambulance. "Ali, maybe there's no reason to . . . Oh, never mind. Stay right here. Don't you move."

She ran over and rapped her knuckles against the back doors of the ambulance. After a moment, the driver poked his head out, and I could see my sister murmuring and gesturing. She glanced back at me and mouthed, "*Stay there*," and disappeared inside.

I realized I was shivering so badly my teeth were chattering, despite the warmth of the morning sun—just like the woman on the curb.

A few moments later, the door to the ambulance opened, and Pearly hurried back. She shook her head when she reached me. A moment later, the ambulance driver emerged alone and headed back toward the fire.

This time the tears came hard. I was sniveling and wiping my nose against my sleeve.

"I know, honey. I know," Pearly soothed. Her hands rubbed my back even as she started urging me to walk. We began to trace the path she'd taken to find me, which skirted the three fires in the area.

"It's horrible," she continued. "And this is just a fraction of it. When you left, I was on the phone with Queen's Hospital. They need doctors and nurses to report to duty. Wounded are coming in from all over, and they need help taking blood donations. Plus, some of us will be headed to Tripler Hospital to help out with the wounded from the bases. We have to get you home, because I've got to get to work."

"What about Papa?" I asked.

"I tried the newspaper, but the lines are busy. I haven't been able to get through to Mama either," answered Pearly.

"Pearly! I didn't even get the emergency supplies. After the explosion, I just . . . dropped everything and left," I said.

"I promise you, Mama is not going to mind," my sister said. "I'm sure she just wants you home safe."

CHAPTER FOUR

Mō'ili'ili, Hawai'i
December 7, 1941
Sunday morning, 11:30 a.m.

The walk back to Pearly's had been sobering. Broken glass, bent pieces of roofing, and debris mingled with toys, books, dishes, clothing, and photo albums, all too burned to recover. Ash-covered people stood dazed in the streets. Firemen rushed between the three fires. And medics treated the wounded under the shade of coconut trees.

"Why isn't there more help?" I asked.

"This is who is available. Most emergency services are needed at Pearl Harbor and the other bases," Pearly said.

Although she hurried me along, she was taking additional glances. I guessed she was trying to decide where she was needed most. Was it here, where her own neighbors were burned and bleeding and shell-shocked? Or was it on the bases, where the damage was much worse?

Back at her apartment, Pearly quickly got dressed in her nurse's uniform and tucked her hair into a simple bun. She did not bother with makeup, instead grabbing her purse and car keys and urging me to her car.

She sped toward Pālolo. The radio sputtered: "The second wave is over. We are now being asked to sign off the air. A third wave is possible. Stay off the streets. Do your best to remain calm."

Mama met us at the street in front of our house. Pearly and I hurried from the car to hug her.

"Everything OK here, Mama?" Pearly asked, concern filling her eyes.

Mama shrugged wearily. "I think so. I'm just trying to keep the kids busy so they don't worry. They're inside doing a puzzle right now."

"Did you hear from Papa?" I asked.

"Not yet," answered Mama. "He must be very busy at work. I'm going to check in after lunch—to see if we should expect him home for supper."

"Yosh is with his ROTC unit. And I hate to rush off, but I am needed at the hospital," Pearly said.

"B-b-but, Pearly, the radio said to stay off the streets," I stammered. Tears threatened to spill. I wanted everyone to stop going. I wanted everyone I loved locked in one small room together until all of this was over.

"Yes, Ali, I know." Pearly looked straight into my eyes. "I wish I could stay here with you." She bit her bottom lip and looked like she might start crying too. "But they need nurses, and I must go. I'll be in touch again as soon as I can. I love you."

She squeezed Mama and me hard. And with that, Pearly drove off.

My arms were still around Mama's waist as we headed back into the house. "I'm so sorry, but I wasn't able to get to Koide Store," I said. "Pearly got called into work so we never went."

I told the lie without having planned to do so. But there was no private space to tell her all I'd seen. Besides I didn't want to upset Mama.

"Never mind, Alice. We have some things left from last hurricane season. It's enough. Maybe we can run to the store tomorrow together. Now, come . . . you should eat. Papa whisked you off before you had your breakfast," she said.

I let Mama fix me a big plate of food and fuss over me and hover. I leaned into my mother's embrace, holding on to her arms a few moments too long. She looked at me quizzically, so I let go and began to eat.

I surprised myself by wolfing down the food. I thought I'd have no appetite, or that I'd be sickened by what I'd seen, but I ate like I was starving.

We were quiet that afternoon. When the radio came back on air, the announcer sternly instructed that martial law had been declared, putting the government of the territory of Hawai'i in the hands of the military. While Momo and Ken played, Mama and I gathered near the radio to listen.

"Starting at six p.m., there will be a curfew and blackout for all residents of Hawai'i territory. No one shall use electricity. All doors and windows must be completely covered in dark material. No one shall leave their home unless they have the proper permit. Schools are now closed until further notice. More directives to follow."

"What does that mean, blackout? And *kerfoo*?" Momo asked.

"*Curfew*," I corrected, but I didn't say anything else because I didn't know.

Mama tilted her head to the side, thinking. "Just that we're going to need to do things a little differently for a while. *Curfew* means we cannot leave the house at nighttime. That's easy—we're almost always home anyway. *Blackout* means we cannot use the lights at night, and we have to put up special curtains. That's OK—maybe we just eat dinner and go to bed earlier."

"I hate the dark. I'm scared of the dark," Momo said, pouting.

"It'll be OK," said Mama. "We can all sleep together. Then you don't have to feel afraid."

Mama and I pulled her mattress down the hall to create a family bed in the room I shared with Momo and Ken. Our bedroom was the farthest from the street, with a side door exit, as well as windows from which we could escape if needed.

When Momo and Ken weren't watching, Mama showed me that she had hid a cleaver and a santoku knife in the top shelf of their dresser. "Just in case," she said.

In case of what? I worried. I remembered Pearly saying she'd heard reports of Japanese pilots in the hills. *Would the enemy show up at our house? And then what? Mama would scare them off with the same cutlery she used to make chicken-fried steak?* I noticed there were two knives and that she'd made sure I knew where they were. *Did she expect me to use one if necessary?*

Not long after we moved the mattress, there came an urgent rapping at our front door. Mama opened the door to two Caucasian policemen. "We're looking for Shiroku Fujii," one said.

Mama said, "He is not here." Her voice had an edge to it, and she used her body to block the doorway from their view.

"Well, where is he?" the man demanded.

"Sorry, I don't know," Mama said.

The second cop's voice was more respectful. "When do you expect him back, ma'am?"

"Again, so sorry, don't know." Her voice was quiet and firm.

"We'll be back," the first cop snapped.

"OK. Is that all?" She waited just long enough for the second man to nod and then shut the door.

She stood a moment, staring at the closed door. Then she nodded to herself, headed to the kitchen, and picked up the phone. She dialed, waited, hung up. Dialed, waited, hung up. Over and again.

CHAPTER FIVE

Pālolo, Hawai'i
December 7, 1941
Sunday afternoon, 3:30 p.m.

"Who are you trying to call, Mama?" I finally asked.

"Papa," she answered. "He should know the police are looking for him."

"Yeah, Mama. How come there were police?" Momo piped up.

Mama shrugged. "I don't know. Maybe it's nothing. Or a misunderstanding. But I don't have a good feeling."

Suddenly the house seemed too large and spooky. Every room Mama entered, we followed.

But when I heard Mama's *tsks* of irritation, I sat Mo and Ken down with me in the living room. There we could watch her disappear and reappear.

A pile grew in the room with us. Kimonos. Books written in Japanese. A white paper parasol with red blossoms on it. The framed lilac-and-gold family crest of wisteria climbing. Momo and Ken fell asleep sitting up on the couch, leaning against my body.

But then Mama began shoving the items into the suitcase, and I could no longer keep quiet. "Why are you packing a suitcase, Mama?" I asked, trying to keep the tremor from my voice.

"If the police come back, Ali, I'm not going to give them anything to find," Mama declared. She began dragging the suitcase outside.

Untangling myself from my sleeping siblings' limbs, I rose to help. Wordlessly we wrestled it down the front stairs and into the small crawl space beneath the porch. There was nothing there but a stray cat that ran off and four large bags of potting soil. We used them to hide the suitcase.

"There," said Mama, wiping her hands on her housedress.

Back in the house, I perched on a kitchen stool while Mama dialed the phone again, waited again, and hung up again. She seemed very discouraged, but she kept trying.

Finally her spine straightened and she began speaking entirely in Japanese. I heard her say "*Shigeo-san, onegai shimasu,*" politely asking to speak to one of Papa's coworkers at *Nippu Jiji*.

After that she spoke too fast for me to follow along with my limited Japanese. I listened as her tone went from questioning to demanding to apologizing.

When Mama hung up the phone, she banged it down hard into its cradle. I winced, waiting for Momo or Ken to wake up, but they didn't.

Looking at a sticky note, Mama picked the phone back up again. "Hello. Mr. Padilla? It's Mrs. Chieko Fujii—Shiroku Fujii's wife . . . Yes, from the Garden Club. How kind of you to remember. May I call on you for a favor? We are selling some bonsai, and I know you are a collector."

Why was she selling Papa's plants? I didn't understand.

"It would be best if you could come today," she said. "As a courtesy, I called you first, but we will have others making offers too. A half hour? OK. You remember where? That's right, Tenth. Past the Number One Store, the driveway after the big mango tree . . . See you then."

After Mama hung up the phone, I whispered, "Why are you selling Papa's plants?"

Mama whispered back, "The police found Papa at *Nippu Jiji*, Ali. They took him in for questioning."

"Questioning!" I cried. "Why? What for?" I was shocked.

"I don't know!" Mama snapped. Then she added, "I'm sorry. I didn't mean to yell. It has something to do with the attack this morning. Which, of course, Papa had nothing to do with. He's not even from Japan. I mean, his parents were, but he was born and raised here. He's an American citizen. If the police had suspicions, you'd think they'd take me instead."

"Why would they want to take you?" I asked, confused.

"Oh, they wouldn't, Ali. Don't worry," she soothed. "I'm just thinking. I'm just surprised they want to question a loyal American citizen over his Japanese immigrant wife."

It frightened me to think about Mama getting questioned too. "But he'll be right back," I insisted. "After they question him. Won't he?"

Mama sighed. "I said I don't know. I hope so. But like I told you, if the police come back, I am not going to give them anything to find. We're good Americans here. No kimonos or Japanese books or bonsai or traitors to be found here . . . "

"OK, Mama. I think I understand," I said. "But please don't sell the Alice."

She paused in the doorway, surprised. "Ali, we need to get rid of *everything*. It's not a safe time to hold on to being Japanese."

"No, Mama. *Not* the Alice. Forgive me, but I will *not* let you sell the Alice." We were both surprised by my stubbornness.

"Such a foolish girl!" Mama stomped her foot hard. "Fine, keep it. But I better not see it. Find a good place to hide it. If I can see it, it's gone."

Mr. Padilla purchased all of Papa's bonsai—all except the Alice, which I had hidden on the roof.

It wasn't a perfect spot since it was now in direct sun and would be hard to water. But Mama would never find it because she was afraid of heights.

After Mr. Padilla left, Mama called the police station, *Nippu Jiji*, the neighbors—whomever she could think of that might know more about Papa. We had been instructed not to make calls unless it was an emergency. But missing family members were an emergency—for us and for others. It was no wonder the lines were busy.

She made little headway beyond the police sergeant who advised, "Ma'am, try to stay calm. You said your husband was taken in for questioning. And you don't understand why he was taken because he is . . . 'a good man.' Well, no doubt once he answers our questions, he'll be home. But it's been a very long day for everyone, and he's not the only one who's been brought in. It won't be more than a couple days at most."

We went to bed early that night—not long after the blackout and curfew had begun. We were exhausted by the sudden strangeness of our lives. I pretended to sleep but tossed and turned. Finally, after a few hours, I crept through the house to fetch the evening edition of *Nippu Jiji* from the porch steps.

The darkness inside the house was smothering. And outside it was darker than I was used to. The streetlights were off, and no car headlights were around to brighten the roads. Instead, the sky was lit by the nearly full moon and more stars than I'd ever noticed.

It might have been beautiful if I wasn't so scared. My senses were sharp. Each rustle of a bush and every shifting shadow changed into an enemy Japanese pilot, hidden in the hills, waiting to strike. I hesitated in the doorway, then made myself go down the steps to grab the newspaper.

I took the paper with me into Papa's office. Huddled in the corner furthest from any windows, I lit one small, forbidden candle and riffled through until I found his byline and began to read.

"Shikataganai: An Opinion" by Shiroku Fujii

In the wise words of our publisher, Mr. Yasutaro Soga, "The fish on the cutting board cannot escape no matter how much it struggles."

This Sunday's stunning attack on Pearl Harbor and its surrounds has brought much sorrow to residents of Hawai'i. The following arrest of many of the pillars of the local Japanese community has been an additional burden for Nikkei to bear.

But right now we must not protest. The smoke still rises. The memory of those red suns burns the eyes. The heart of the land beats painfully.

The best way to help our home—by which, allow me to be clear, I mean Hawai'i—is to obey and remain calm. If the Americans doubt our loyalty, let us prove it. Make the sacrifice to accept the current sentence of being Japanese. Endure. Persevere. And by so doing, take pride in our resilience as citizens of this fine territory.

I lay the paper on Papa's desk, tiptoed back to our bedroom, and crawled in bed next to my mama. She didn't wake, but her soft body shifted to curve around mine.

CHAPTER SIX

Pālolo, Hawai'i
December 8, 1941
Monday morning, 8 a.m.

When I woke the next day, I woke to war.

In the kitchen, over a breakfast of cold rice and eggs drizzled with soy sauce, Mama told us that President Roosevelt had declared war against Japan. She'd heard it on the radio earlier that morning.

I pushed my food around my plate and worried. *Japan shocked us! They outsmarted America, and now we're going to war with them. What does "war" mean? Will the Japanese attack again? If they do, I think they'll go for more than just planes and ships. Will they take over the islands?*

I imagined more ghostship planes, more smoke and big sounds, more destruction and death. I didn't think I could bear not ever knowing whether we were safe.

When I looked at Momo and Ken, I thought of the little girl from the ambulance. And thinking of her while looking at them made my stomach hurt so much I thought I might throw up.

We hadn't heard from Papa, Pearly, or Yosh. With schools closed, Momo and Ken followed me like shadows. We dared not leave our house.

Questions filled my head. Papa had written, "But right now we must not protest." *Well, why not? Why must we obey and remain calm?* I wondered.

I felt like the worst daughter ever because, left alone with my questions, the one that I tried hardest to drown out still came through as a snide whisper: *Did Papa do something wrong?*

As soon as the question formed, I silenced it: *No. He was questioned because he works for a Japanese newspaper! Because he is a respected leader of the Japanese community!*

And that same snide whisper would ask, *So, he's well connected? Quite the network, then?*

I tried to strangle the voice. How could I doubt my papa? How could I think so little of someone I loved so much? How could anyone think that he could be the enemy?

A knock on the door that afternoon sent Momo and Ken scurrying for cover. Mama and I exchanged a look, worried it was the policemen returning. But when Mama opened the door, it was Mrs. Midori from down the block. She carried a container of beef stew.

"Oh, Yuki, you shouldn't have. You are too kind," Mama said.

I could tell from her pink cheeks that Mama was embarrassed by the generosity. It did smell faintly of charity.

OK, so people know about Papa being taken for questioning, then, I thought. *Mama's a single parent and we're practically orphans, deserving of beef stew with fresh chunks of pity in it.*

But Mrs. Midori drowned out my mother's embarrassed protests. She quickly replied, "We made too much. It's just leftovers. Anyway, it's not as good as your stew."

Mama sent us kids from the room. "Alice, put them down for a nap, and finish folding the laundry on my bed," she said.

I nodded, happy to have something to focus on besides my worries about war and my missing family members. It felt good to have a problem before me I could actually solve, even if it was simply folding a load of white towels and clothing.

Momo and Ken curled up at the head of our parents' bed and soon nodded off due to boredom and the quiet. Once I was sure they were asleep, I slipped from the room to put away the freshly folded towels.

The sliding door in the kitchen was open, and I could hear Mama and Mrs. Midori speaking in low murmurs.

"The sergeant said he'd be a few days, but I just don't know," Mama whispered. My stomach clenched to hear my mother so uncertain. *Was she talking about Papa?*

"I am truly sorry, Chieko-san," Mrs. Midori comforted her.

"What am I supposed to do?" Mama asked. "When will Shiroku be home? What if the money runs out? I'll have three kids to support. At least Pearly and Yosh can fend for themselves."

It hurt my heart to hear Mama's private worries.

The policeman said a few days. Why does she seem to think it will be longer? I wondered. *How much money do we have saved? When will it run out? And why doesn't she share these worries with me? Why does she share them with the first neighbor to bring her some stew?*

Mrs. Midori replied, "It won't come to that. But even if it did, Pearly and Yosh will help. They're good kids."

As they kept talking, I started a mental list of how I could help with money. *I could babysit. I could get an after-school job at the pineapple cannery. We could sell some of our more valuable things.*

"But I can't get ahold of them," Mama said. "Not since yesterday when Pearly dropped Alice off. She was headed to work at Queen's, and Yosh had already left with his ROTC unit. They were safe then, but now the phone just rings and rings."

"Their help is needed. Otherwise they'd be here." Mrs. Midori's voice was firm. "You Fujiis are close. It's one of the things I've admired most about your family."

"You're very kind to say so," Mama replied.

I found myself smiling, also liking this vision Mrs. Midori painted of us.

"Honestly, I'm jealous," teased Mrs. Midori. "Me and Isamu only have each other, and some days we're not even sure we like each other."

Mama laughed. "I think every marriage is like that, Yuki. Shiroku makes me so furious sometimes. But I tell you what. The Hawaiians sometimes adopt friends into their family, right? So we will adopt you too. I will hold fast to your good friendship."

"That is a great comfort to me," Mrs. Midori said. "In any case, I am certain that Pearly and Yosh are safe and will get in touch soon. Your mother's heart would tell you if they were harmed."

"You must be right. My mind just cannot stop," Mama replied. "But listen to me, going on about my trouble. I am ashamed. How are you and Isamu faring?"

Mrs. Midori groaned. "Well, he is upset with me right now. I told him he had to get rid of the birds because somebody will think we used them to send messages to the enemy. Foolish man, he tried to free them. They came right back—they're homing pigeons! All morning, he's in tears, begging the birds to fly away. I knew I had to protect us both because Isamu's too soft. So I did away with them myself."

I balled a fist to my mouth. *Those poor lovely birds.* I hated Mrs. Midori. *How could she?*

"It was awful. . . ." Mrs. Midori started to cry.

Now Mama comforted Mrs. Midori. "You did what you had to," she said. "It was the right thing."

Mrs. Midori's voice turned hard. "I *know* it was the right thing. I did what he *should* have. I left him home to bury them and break down the cages. It's pointless, though. Everyone knows we kept those birds, and they're going to twist it somehow and make us out to be spies. I just know it. They'll say we were using the birds to pass messages to enemy Japanese. Truth is, Isamu kept those birds because he loved them like they were his children." Mrs. Midori was silent a moment and then in a small voice said, "It's just a matter of time before they come for Isamu. Maybe me too."

"Oh, Yuki." Mama sighed. "Stay strong, ne? Take care of Isamu but also yourself. . . ."

At that moment I shifted my weight, and the floorboard creaked under me. And I was glad it had. I had thought I wanted to know everything, but now I had no idea what to do with all that information. And I didn't want to think about the possibility of the police coming for more of us, just because we happened to be Japanese.

"So, ne . . . you must give me your recipe." Mrs. Midori's voice was a notch louder, as if I was supposed to believe they'd been trading recipes for the past half hour.

I poked my head into the kitchen. "*Gomenasai*," I apologized in Japanese. "I . . . uh . . . was just about to put away the towels."

"Momo and Ken?" Mama asked.

"Napping," I answered.

Mrs. Midori stood and gently pushed in her chair. "I better go. It's getting late." She bowed to Mama. "Tell me anytime if there's anything I can do that would help."

"And you as well, Yuki. Anytime," Mama said, warmly embracing Mrs. Midori before she left.

CHAPTER SEVEN

Waikiki, Hawai'i
December 28, 1941
Sunday morning, 10 a.m.

The days following the attack passed like dominoes falling. Each day brought new rules: gas and food rationing, censoring of newspapers and radio programs, monitoring of postal mail and phone conversations, the suspension of *Nippu Jiji* and other Japanese-language newspapers.

Mama eventually got a hold of Yosh and Pearly, but she couldn't learn anything more about Papa. All the authorities would do was confirm that he was helping and had been moved to Sand Island Detention Center.

Christmas came and went—our first without Papa. None of us felt very jolly, except perhaps Momo and Ken. But we hung tinsel and a few glass bulbs on the plumeria tree in the front yard, and Mama made sure there was a new book, a hand-knitted pair of socks, and a juicy Ka'u gold orange in each of our stockings.

Papa had now been gone three weeks. Slowly, horribly, I was becoming used to him being gone. I had begun to understand that Papa was being held because he was the kind of good man—good, *Japanese* man—who was the backbone of his family and community. He had been taken *because* he gave the community strength.

Shortly after Christmas, we got hit by a day so hot it made the house feel like an oven. Mama wasn't much of a beach person, but Momo, Ken, and I piled into Pearly's car and headed to our favorite beach, *Sans Souci*.

Sans Souci, French for “no worries,” was where we’d learned to swim. The idea was to take our minds off things and escape the heat.

While Pearly parked, Momo and Ken and I barreled toward the sea. But today there was no getting our minds off things—barbed wire was strung along the shoreline, and the grassy field was crisscrossed with soldiers in uniform, heading to train there.

Pearly caught up with us at the grass’s edge. “Catch!” she said, tossing me four towels.

She grabbed Momo and Ken’s hands and took off running across the sand. Just above where the water lapped the beach, she dumped out a few buckets and small shovels from the bag slung over her shoulder. As Momo and Ken reached for their toys, Pearly stripped down to her suit. It was a teal one-piece with a triangle cutout in the middle to show off her stomach.

"Pearly! Mama would *kill* you if she saw you in that!" I said.

"Well, Alice," she replied, shimmying a shoulder, "it's a good thing Mama never goes to the beach then."

I giggled and laid out the four towels. I stripped down too, but my swimsuit was more plain—dark blue with a high, rounded neckline and a flared skirt. Next to Pearly's, it was a little girl's suit.

Ken-chan was sitting in the waves, nearly getting bowled over between his laughs. Where the dry sand met the wet, Momo was carving and smoothing, digging and shaping.

I kneeled down beside her and asked, "What are you making? Can I help?"

Soon both Ken and I were drawn into a detailed plan for a sand zoo. I would build sturdy walls and gates, and Momo would fill them with seashell animals.

Ken's job was to fill his bucket with wet sand and deliver it back. "Don't touch nothing," Momo ordered him, "or I'll give you lickin's!"

"That's not nice, Momo," I chided.

"Sorry," she said. "But he better not mess up my zoo."

I dug canals to head off incoming waves. To strengthen the outside walls, I supported the damp sand with driftwood. Soon three walls stood against the beating waves. The fourth wall I would leave till later, since Momo was kneeling in its space, placing the animals in their homes.

I looked over my sand-covered self. "Momo, I gotta rinse off. I'll be right back." She nodded.

I headed to the water and dove in. I came up only when I needed air. Emerging from the water, I wrung out my dripping hair and scanned the beach. I spotted some schoolmates. Three girls and two boys.

“Helen! Diane! Maile!” I called and headed over, glancing back to make sure my siblings were safe.

I knew the boys’ names too, but I didn’t call to them. I might not have gone over, though, if Abe Akaka hadn’t been there. Abe, whose smile melted me. At the end of sixth grade, he’d been just one of many chubby Asian boys with a bowl haircut. But something had happened over the summer. Abe entered seventh grade a foot taller—or so it seemed—and was now lean and tanned.

I didn’t know Diane or Maile well—all I knew about Diane was that she was from a military family. But Helen lived just a few blocks from me, and we’d been close when we were younger. Now, though, as she shaded her face to look up at me, I felt I was looking at a stranger. It wasn’t just that she and the other girls had bathing suits closer to Pearly’s; it was her dull eyes.

"Oh. Hey, Alice," Helen replied. She flipped onto her stomach and picked up her book.

Maile, already lying on her stomach, glanced up at our exchange. Diane, lounging on her back, propped herself up on her elbows to see me better. "Alice? Alice *Fuji*?"

She had mangled my family name into a mountain and an apple, but I nodded. "It's *Fujii*, not *Fuji*, but pretty close." I smirked at Abe and his friend Johnny. I liked this version of myself: bold, funny, not shy. What else was she capable of?

"*Fuji* or *Fujii*—anyway, what are *you* doing here?" Diane replied. "We're at war, don't you know? And you Japs are the enemy."

Suddenly it felt like I could hear each palm branch as it rustled in the trade winds and each wave as it raked over shells and pebbles. Maile and Helen were as still as mannequins. Abe and Johnny didn't meet my eyes, but I knew they'd heard.

I sucked in a long breath, crossing my arms at my chest. I ignored Diane and turned to my childhood friend. "Helen?"

Helen kept still, then shrugged, just barely.

"Seriously, Helen? You agree with this . . . base brat?" I spat the words out. "You think *I'm* the enemy?"

I absolutely couldn't look away from Helen, though my eyes stung from the effort not to blink. The tips of her ears turned red with embarrassment.

"And what about *Maile*?" I was livid. "*I'm* the enemy, but she's not? She's Hawaiian-Filipino, but she's part 'Jap' too!"

"Her dad didn't get arrested on the same day that Pearl Harbor was attacked, Al." Helen's voice was calm and cold, which made the use of her old nickname for me more painful.

"He didn't get arrested! He was detained by the . . . he got taken for . . . ," I sputtered helplessly.

"Alice, hon, it's time to go home." Pearly had approached without me noticing. Her sandy towel was tucked around her hips. Her voice was sweet, and her smile bright and wide, but it didn't reach her eyes.

I let Pearly take my arm, but before I'd taken five steps, I whirled around. "Helen . . ." I didn't wait for her to respond or even look up. "It could just as easily have been you. If it had been China bombing the harbor, *you* would have been the Japs."

CHAPTER EIGHT

Pālolo, Hawai'i
March 2, 1942
Monday morning, 8 a.m.

On the first Monday of March, I was back to school for the first time in almost three months. The desks were dusty, and they seemed smaller. Maybe it was because our seats were crowded with the gas masks and heavy oxygen canisters we now had to carry. We had to be prepared in case of an air raid or poison gas attack.

I couldn't concentrate. I missed Momo and Ken and Mama. How could we be sure it was safe to be back to school? It felt wrong to be away from them.

It was like a first day of school. Girls wore nice dresses with their hair carefully arranged. Boys wore crisp new shirts. I felt shy, embarrassed, and nervous. Like I knew no one and no one knew me.

A bell rang. We all had to hurry to secure our strange masks over our faces while teachers tested the fit.

The mask blurred my vision and made my breaths feel shallow, as if each was bouncing around inside the mask like a ping-pong ball. Wearing it, I felt panicked, but in another way, safe. Behind the mask, I didn't have to hide how lonely I felt. With the masks on, no one was Japanese. We all looked the same—like alien children.

When we broke for recess, I opened a book and pretended to read while the others filed past. I hadn't hung out with anyone I wasn't related to since the day at *Sans Souci*. The last thing I wanted to do was go outside and have no one to talk to.

Someone paused a moment by my desk, said, “Hey,” and touched my hand.

I looked up. It was Johnny Lum Lee, Abe’s friend from the beach. He had his mask and oxygen canister slung over his shoulder.

“Hey,” I replied.

“Alice *Fuji*, right? Like the apple?” He emphasized my last name in imitation of the way Diane had that day at the beach.

“Ha. Ha.” I gave him my best stink eye.

“Kidding!” Johnny laughed. I hadn’t noticed his dimples before. “Anyway . . . haven’t seen you since—”

“Since Diane kindly informed me that I’m ‘the enemy’?” I asked.

“Good thing she told you. Poor thing, you didn’t know.” Johnny put a hand on my shoulder. “Come on, *Apple*,” he said. “Grab your mask and tank. Let’s go outside.”

Outside, the schoolyard had been transformed. In the middle of the wide yard where we'd played dodgeball and run laps, trenches had been dug. Even in the fresh air, I felt short of breath. War had painted over the surface of every single thing I had ever enjoyed.

Johnny led me over to where Abe and Maile had gathered. Abe was so good looking I couldn't look straight at him. I had to force myself to find words.

"Hey, Maile," I finally said. "I'm really sorry about the other day. You know, calling you a Jap."

She laughed. "No worries, Alice. You've got nothing to be sorry for. Heat of the moment."

"My mom would say it's the pot calling the kettle black," Abe said. "Doesn't sting—"

Abe's words were cut off by a siren wail. It quickly became higher and louder.

"Masks on. In the trenches. Hustle!" our teacher, Mr. Wright, bellowed.

Putting my mask on, I ran like I was racing across burning sand. Abe and Johnny were fast, but I was close on their heels as we vaulted into the trench.

Not enough air. Heart pounding. Cemented feet. Swarm of hornets inside. By now I recognized these steps toward a panic attack, even if I didn't know how to make it stop.

Abe and Johnny were slumped against the wall, and for a moment I thought they'd been hit by something I hadn't heard coming. I thought of the woman I'd seen months ago, bleeding on the street: *The window just went explode. No warning.*

Other boys were jumping in now too, all wearing the masks, which terrified me all over again, even though I knew I was wearing the same thing. I simply could not catch my breath.

I ripped off my gas mask and moved toward Abe and Johnny. That was when the boys turned to me. No blood. Their bodies whole and unhurt. They quickly removed their masks.

"Whoa, Apple," Johnny said, his eyes wide. "You OK? Catch your breath, sistah."

With a feather-light touch, Abe smoothed my hair. “It was just a drill, Alice,” he said quietly.

“Yeah, I know that,” I said. “Of course.”

You did not know that, but somehow they knew that, I thought. *Will I ever stop feeling scared?*

CHAPTER NINE

Pālolo, Hawaiʻi
March 8, 1942
Sunday afternoon, 5:30 p.m.

"So, how is it being back to school, Ali?" Yosh asked. It was the first Sunday after I had returned to school. Mama, Yosh, Pearly, Momo, Ken, and I had gathered for a family dinner. Early Sunday dinners, planned with plenty of time before blackout and curfew, were part of our new normal.

Yosh and Pearly were preparing chicken katsu, and I was chopping cherry tomatoes for a salad. Momo and Ken sat on stools pulled up to the counter and sneaked tomatoes. Mama was writing letters at the dining room table.

"It's strange," I admitted. "I mean, seventh grade already was strange. Like, everyone's running around falling in love with each other and then breaking up, or being best, best friends and then the next week hating each other. But you add gas masks and air-raid drills, and it just gets weirder. You know, the first air-raid drill, I didn't even know it was a drill. I was terrified. Everything feels so *dramatic*. Like we're just one big blob of *emotions*."

I sighed and slid the cutting board's load into a wooden bowl. Pearly had already layered romaine ribbons, cucumber half-moons, sweet wedges of tangerine, and tiny, firm cubes of tofu.

"Hormones, sis," Yosh said, laughing, as he sliced the chicken.

Pearly piped up. "What I want to know is who do you love? And who loves you?" She dressed the salad with drizzles of sesame oil, soy sauce, and rice vinegar.

"Oh, it's not like that," I said. But I thought of how I couldn't even look at Abe and of how easy it was to talk to Johnny. "I mean the stuff about emotions for girls too. Like, girls can be friends and then they don't talk for half a year, and it's like they never knew each other at all."

"Like Helen." Pearly sighed as she rummaged through the fridge.

"Helen Chang?" Mama called from the living room. "What happened with Helen?" She brought the letter she was working on and sat down at the table with us.

"It was that day we went to the beach, Ma," Pearly answered. She emerged from the fridge with the ketchup, Worcestershire sauce, and oyster sauce she needed to make katsu sauce. "Back in early January? Alice had a run-in with Helen and some classmates who said not-very-nice things about Papa and being Japanese."

"It's funny, though," I said, as I watched Pearly stir those ingredients in a large glass bowl with a few spoonfuls of sugar. "If that terrible day hadn't happened, school would be even worse for me. It's because of that day that I made some friends."

"Friends are known first in hardship," Mama said, nodding.

"What?" I asked. "Where'd that bit of wisdom come from?"

"Maybe a fortune cookie?" Yosh joked.

"Hush up, you smart mouths," scolded Mama. "It's something your *Obasan* used to say. Anyone can be friendly when life is easy. It's when things get tough that you find your true friends. I've thought about this a lot. About who came by after Papa got taken away and who didn't. Who was loyal and who was scared that our bad luck was contagious. Believe me, I *noticed*."

Mama held up the papers on which she'd been writing and added, "This letter I'm writing? It's for Mrs. Midori. I didn't tell you, but she and Mr. Midori got taken to Sand Island last week."

Pearly and Yosh *tsked* and shook their heads, but this news didn't faze them. They kept preparing plates of food. But despite everything I'd been through, I could still be shocked.

"What?" I exclaimed. Part of me still hated Mrs. Midori for killing the birds. But even so, she didn't deserve to be locked up. "I can't believe it. Why?"

"The birds," Mama said. "Just as she feared."

Yosh and Pearly handed out full plates and chopsticks. In front of me was a mound of white rice, golden strips of breaded chicken, rich reddish brown katsu sauce, and the colorful salad I'd made with Pearly. The fragrant steam rose from the food. Everything had been perfectly made, but now I wasn't sure I'd be able to eat a bite.

"So let me get this right. The Midoris got arrested because they had pet birds that someone thought could be used to pass secret spy messages? What's next? Will they arrest someone for having binoculars or a camera?" I said, my voice shaky.

"Actually they probably *would* arrest them since all Japanese had to turn over those kinds of things to the authorities on December seventh. Cameras, binoculars, shortwave radios, guns . . . ," Yosh said. "It'd look pretty fishy if you held onto any of that."

"Ugh!" I stomped my foot in frustration. "You know what I *mean*, Yosh. What did Mrs. Midori do wrong?" I turned to Mama. "What's the difference between her and you, Mama? How do we know you're not next?"

I had voiced my very worst fear. Things were hard enough. More than one night, I'd lost hours of sleep trying to picture my life if a knock at the door were to take away Mama too.

"Why don't they just round us all up and get it over with?" I said.

"Be careful what you wish for, Ali," Yosh said. He was quiet a moment, watching Momo and Ken, who seemed to be tuning us out. Then he lowered his voice and said, “You hear about Executive Order 9066? They’ve started evacuating anyone with Japanese ancestry in California, Oregon, Washington, and Arizona. Rounding them up into ‘relocation camps’ further inland. The military says it’s to protect the Japanese and to allow them to prove their loyalty.”

Even in the humid afternoon, I felt a chill down my spine hearing my big brother’s words.

Yosh continued, “People are being given just a few days to pack, store, or sell everything they own. They can only bring with them what they can carry in their own two hands. Their neighbors pick through the things they can’t pack and offer to buy them for just pennies. Or worse, they come just to look and then come back and take things for free once the families have left. It’s disgusting. There’s even talk of closing Sand Island in O‘ahu and moving internees to mainland camps.”

Mama had been quiet, letting the conversation volley between Pearly, Yosh, and me, but she spoke now. "Sometimes I wonder if that would be better. What Ali said. Round us all up. Get it over with. I miss Papa. My life here is so different than when I was growing up in Japan. At least if we were in camps, we'd be together. I could put up with a lot, if only I were able to draw on Papa's strength."

I understood what she meant. I felt stronger when I was with my family. But I also felt betrayed by her. *I'm thirteen, my whole life's ahead of me*, I thought. *I've only started making friends, and you're willing to rip all that from me just to be back with Papa?*

CHAPTER TEN

Sand Island, Honolulu, Hawai'i
June 17, 1942
Wednesday morning, 9 a.m.

At the end of May, we received a notice in the mail saying that families would be allowed to visit Sand Island internees twice a month. Our first visit was scheduled for mid-June.

It had been more than six months since Pearl Harbor was attacked and Papa had been taken. Mama had made phone calls every day, but none of us had seen or spoken to him since that day in December.

The air was moist and humid on the islands on June 17, when the five of us arrived at Sand Island Detention Center.

We were all freshly scrubbed and wearing bright dresses or pressed pants and button-down shirts. Other visitors were arriving, similarly dressed up. A few women were alone, but other women led children of various ages.

Uniformed soldiers holding bayonets ushered us all into a building in front of the camp headquarters. For a brief moment, I wondered if we were going to see Papa at all or if this was just another step in the round-up of people with our kind of faces.

We sat at long tables, fidgeting under the gaze of a lieutenant. While we sat, I thought about how Papa would have to pass beyond the barbed wire that strung the camp's boundaries.

The sound of shuffling feet quieted us. A soldier entered the building, saluting the lieutenant, and then the men filed in. I thought I recognized a few, but I wasn't sure because they were all sunburnt deep brown, unshaven, and in tattered clothes.

Before I'd even picked Papa out of the lineup, the lieutenant announced the beginning of visiting hours. The men hurried to rejoin their families. The room filled with exclamations and chatter in both Japanese and English.

A salt-haired, darker-skinned Papa hugged Mama tightly. Mama's back shuddered a moment before she stepped back, pushing Momo and Ken forward.

"Little peach, how you've grown!" he cried. "Ken-chan! Such a big boy!"

Momo and Ken smiled at him, but they were uncertain smiles, the kind they gave to strangers. We'd waited so long see Papa. Now that we were here, it felt awkward and wrong.

I did the only thing I could think of and exclaimed, "Puppy pile!" I pulled Momo and Ken into a hug with Papa. Yosh smashed himself, Pearly, and a protesting Mama in as well.

It was just the thing to melt whatever had been holding us apart. We turned back into our family.

"Thank you for that puppy pile, Ali-chan." Papa gave me a special extra squeeze. He sat down at the table next to Mama, and Ken-chan sat on her lap. The rest of us sat on the opposite side.

"Now, tell me . . . Ali, Yosh, Momo . . . how is school?" Papa started. "School is important, yeah? Ali-chan, are you taking good care of Momo-chan and Ken-chan? And Pearly and Yosh, are you taking good care of Alice and Mama?"

We nodded. Momo complained about a bossy girl at her school, which made Papa wink at the rest of us as we hid our smiles. Pearly relayed that she was in high demand as a nurse—although some patients had refused to be tended by a "Jap." Yosh beamed as he told Papa that he had joined the Varsity Victory Volunteers to provide manual labor and assist the Army in whatever way they saw fit.

"Right after the attack on Pearl Harbor, all ROTC got drafted into the Hawai'i Territorial Guard, they called it. I couldn't even call home, but I was ready to fight," Yosh said. "There were rumors of spies in the hills, so they gave us guns and had us staking out. We never even got training. Then they went and changed their mind and kicked all the Japanese out of the Guard. Ho, I was *mad* at first. But then I thought about it. Eh, they want to call us spies? Bad Americans? Well, I want to prove them wrong. I'm going to help the Army any way I can."

"I'm very proud of you." Papa said.

"You're not mad?" I asked. "He's helping the people who put you in prison!"

"Gee, thanks a lot, sis . . . ," Yosh muttered. But he bumped my shoulder playfully.

"No, Alice," Papa replied, ignoring Yosh's interjection. "I'm not mad. And I'm not a *prisoner*, I'm an *internee*."

I banged the table. “What’s the difference?” I cried. “You can’t come home! We haven’t even seen you in six months! Papas are supposed to be home with their families. It isn’t fair!”

The soldiers with their bayonets glanced up at my raised voice.

“Alice, watch your tone with your father, and remember where you are,” Mama scolded in a fierce whisper.

“It’s OK, Chieko,” Papa reassured Mama.

We all were quiet a moment. When Papa spoke again, it was with a lowered voice. “Look, Ali, I get it. It doesn’t make sense. No one would choose this,” he said, holding his hands wide. “But we each have to do what is in our power to do. You can bang your fists and yell about fairness. But all you have is sore hands, no breath, and a loss of dignity. You cannot always control what happens to you, but you can always choose how you react.”

“The bamboo that bends is stronger than the oak that resists,” Mama said. Then she hurried to add, “And no! It’s not from a fortune cookie!”

Papa looked puzzled while the rest of us laughed.

“The kids have been teasing me for quoting Japanese proverbs, but what can I say?” Mama continued. “I’m not a writer like you, Papa. All I can do is repeat the things my parents and grandparents would say to me while I was growing up. *Friends are known in hardship. The nail that sticks out will get hammered down.* Those words were good enough for them and for me. They guided me back to my values when I got too hotheaded and forgot. Values shape the character, remind you that who you want to be is a choice. *Fall down seven times—*”

Papa chimed in with her, “*—stand up eight.*”

We continued to talk for a while before Papa said, "Now, hold on, before I forget . . ."

He had put down a paper bag when he first sat down with us. He reached into it now, pulling out cellophane-wrapped butterscotches and peppermints to share with us.

"And this is for Mama." Papa held up a handmade necklace, a huge perfect 'opihi shell strung on a piece of thin yarn, as if its maker had unraveled a sweater to create it. "It's from Yuki Midori. She's very grateful for the care packages you've been sending, Chieko-san. She speaks glowingly of you. I had no idea you were so close."

"It happened after you were taken. But yes, she's a wonderful friend. I think of her like a sister." Mama fingered the perfect 'opihi shell with a soft smile on her face.

I had a gift of my own. From under the table, I brought forth the Alice.

"Oh, Alice." Papa wept. "I can't believe . . ."

The plant had lived on our roof these six months, in heavy rain and steady sun. I often forgot she was up there, and she would go without watering till I remembered.

The tree was no longer blooming, weeds had taken root at its base, the branches no longer formed the perfect parasol, and the leaves were not as healthy as they once were. It had a wild, scrappy look to it, but the Alice was determined to thrive.

As was I. So much had happened in the past half year. I'd turned thirteen. I'd run through flame-lined streets, scared for my life, while the ground shook beneath my feet and the sky above flashed with gunfire. I'd had nearly every part of my life changed by martial law. I'd experienced the ways that fear slid easily into hatred and prejudice. I'd observed too, the way, as Mama had put it, that friends are known first in hardship.

I'd come to know that ache for missing loved ones, the dull pain of never knowing whether they were safe. I'd learned to live with so many unanswered questions.

On the one hand, I understood that at any moment the rug could again be pulled from beneath my feet. But on the other hand, I'd come to see that the only thing I could count on was change.

I was still waiting for things to come out right in the end, as Papa had promised. But I had faith and hope. I had already weathered so much, just like Papa's bonsai. I felt strong and brave. I could wait a little longer.

"Sorry, Papa," I said. "I know she's seen better days."

"No, Alice," whispered Papa. "She's perfect."

A NOTE FROM THE AUTHOR

The December 7, 1941, attack on Pearl Harbor was one of the most terrible acts of war ever committed against the United States. When it was all over, 2,403 Americans had died, and more than 1,000 people were wounded. In comparison, Japan lost 55 men. The next day, the United States declared war on Japan and entered World War II.

Many new rules were put in place under martial law. For example, all Hawai‘i residents had to stay home and darken their windows at night; in case another attack came from Japan, the lack of light would make it harder for pilots to find the islands. Everyone had to carry ID cards and gas masks at all times. Schools were temporarily closed. Food, supplies, and gasoline were rationed. Radio shows, newspapers, phone calls, and postal mail were all watched and reviewed by the military government.

There were even more rules for "enemy aliens"—mostly Japanese and Japanese Americans, as well as some Germans and Italians. These groups were forced to give up anything that might be used to help "the enemy": cameras, portable radios, flashlights, and firearms. Because of rules about where "enemy aliens" could live and work, some found themselves without jobs and land. For example, "enemy aliens" could not work as fishermen, since officials feared they were spying out on the sea.

When I began researching this event, I was already familiar with some parts of the story. I grew up on O'ahu, so I had even gone on school field trips to the WWII memorial at the *USS Arizona*, a ship sunk during the attack. Also, I am half-Japanese, and I knew about the internment of Japanese and Japanese Americans on the mainland. After President Roosevelt ordered "all persons of Japanese ancestry" to report for incarceration, my maternal grandparents were interned. Though both had been living in Sacramento, California, they actually met in Arkansas, at Camp Jerome. They were among the 120,000 men, women, and children of Japanese ancestry that were evicted from the U.S. west coast and imprisoned in camps.

That said, in my family, questions about the war and the internment were mostly met with "*shikata ga nai*"—it cannot be helped—often said with impatience. *Look,* they seemed to say. *It was war, nothing can be done about it, and also hush up because look at this great American life we're living now. Never mind the past.*

As I researched, I was often surprised by how the attack had affected Japanese and Japanese American lives. I had thought it was just Pearl Harbor that had been attacked—but that was not true at all. I had heard that the racial hatred experienced on the U.S. mainland hadn't touched the islands, since by that time Japanese made up forty percent of the total population—but that wasn't exactly true. I had understood that no one in Hawai'i was interned—but that wasn't true either.

In fact, from December 7, 1941, onward, 1,569 people were quietly arrested in Hawai'i, 1,444 of whom were either Japanese nationals or Japanese Americans. You read that right: on the same day of the Pearl Harbor attack, the new martial government that had just been put in power began making arrests. The arrests moved quickly because the government already had made lists of important Japanese and Japanese American community leaders, as early as 1935.

As I read deeper into the past surrounding Pearl Harbor, I slowly began to fill the gaps in my knowledge. But it was my family's quiet determination, grace, and ability to endure that moved and inspired me as I wrote.

My hope, dear reader, is that you are whisked off to 1940s Hawai'i and can feel the salt, sun, and trade winds. I hope Alice grows in your heart like her namesake bonsai tree. I hope you can see yourself in her and know that you too, are strong just like her. You are *resilient*. Do you know that word? If not, you're going to learn it today. It means

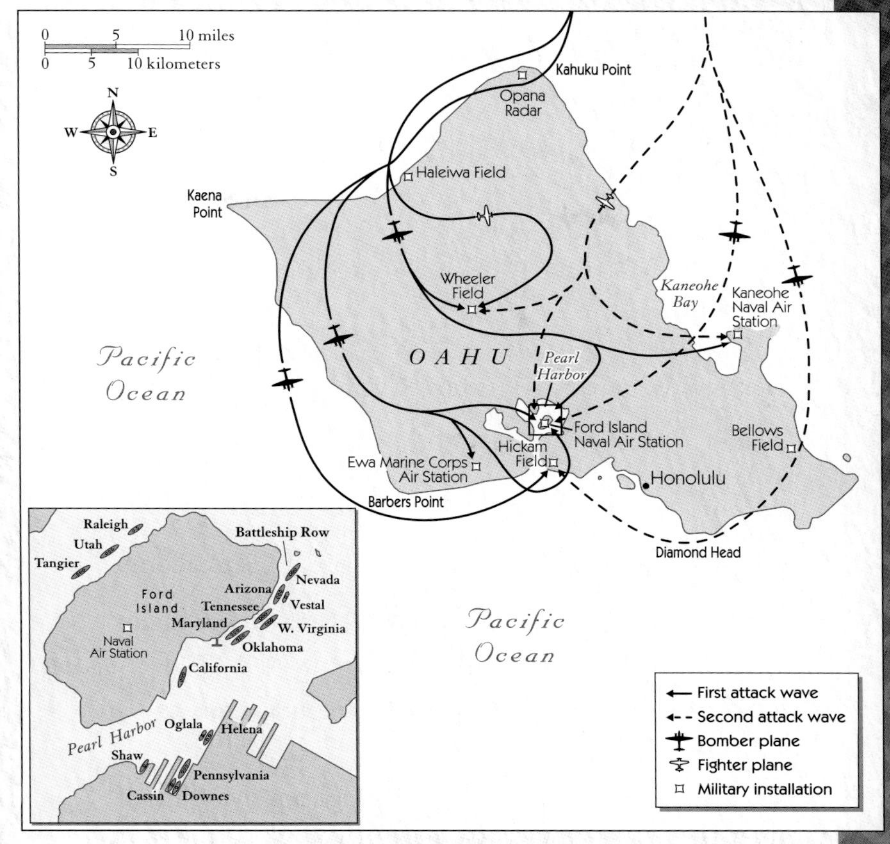

A map shows the December 7, 1941, attack on the island of O'ahu.

"able to bounce back" . . . but not just that. It means knowing that you are more than your home situation, your report card, your spot at a lunch table, your mistakes, even more than your proudest achievements. It means believing that no matter how awful things seem, they will get better, you are not alone, and you can always, always, always rise up again.

GLOSSARY

bayonets (BAY-uh-nets)—long knives that can be fastened to the end of a rifle

bonsai (bon-sye)—a miniature tree or shrub grown in a pot by special methods to restrict its growth; also the art of growing such a plant

censoring (SEN-ser-ing)—removing parts of a publication thought to be harmful or offensive to the public

dignity (DIG-nuh-tee)—the quality of being worthy of honor and respect

directives (duh-REK-tivs)—instructions from a high-level body or official

homing pigeons (HOH-ming PIJ-uhns)—birds trained to deliver messages and return home

internees (in-tur-NEES)—people who are confined to a certain area by force, especially during war

kimonos (kim-MOH-nohs)—long, loose robes with wide sleeves and a sash, worn in Japan

maneuver (muh-NOO-ver)—a training exercise by armed forces

martial law (MAHR-shuhl LAW)—rule by the army in time of war or disaster

military drill (MIL-uh-ter-ee DRIL)—a training exercise for members of the military

persevere (pur-suh-VEER)—to keep trying without giving up even in the face of obstacles or difficulties

protest (pro-TEST)—to object to something strongly and publicly

rationing (RASH-uhn-ing)—controlling the amount one can use

resilience (ri-ZIL-yuhns)—the ability to recover from or adjust to misfortune or change

ROTC (ahr-oh-tee-SEE)—abbreviation for Reserve Officers' Training Corps, a group of students at some colleges and universities who are given training toward becoming officers in the armed forces

shell-shocked (SHEL SHOKD)—feeling very anxious and worried following a battle or attack

snide (SNIDE)—slyly uncomplimentary or insulting

suspension (suh-SPEN-shuhn)—the act of stopping something for a certain amount of time

MAKING CONNECTIONS

1. Alice survived several events and hardships during the book. Compare and contrast two or three of them.

2. One of this book's themes is that family can help you through difficult times. Explain how the family members help each other.

3. Pretend you are Alice and write a letter to your father at Sand Island. Remember your letter will be read and censored by officials.

ABOUT THE AUTHOR

Mayumi Shimose Poe grew up in Hawai'i. Before she could even read, she dictated books to her mother and started her own lending library, complete with laminated membership cards and increasingly dire return reminders. She lives with her husband and two sons in Los Angeles, where she writes stories and works as an editor. Learn more at mayumishimosepoewriter.com.